THE FLATCOAT FABLES

CONTENTS

XII ~

This book is dedicated to the dogs
who shared their lives with us:
Flatcoated Retrievers Saga, Folly and Epic,
who provided the inspiration for this book.
Also to Whimsey (yellow Labrador Retriever),
and Fable (Golden Retriever) the memory of whom
helped me to differentiate between retriever breeds

Friends and family have had to put up with me
constructing The Fables and acting out the thoughts
of Saga and Folly in The Logs, I can only apologize
for any distress or ennui caused thereby!

I am immensely grateful to Rieko Mamaoto
for her charming drawings and to Nikita Ogurtsov
for redrawing the illustrations to make them
'book ready'; and for the wonderful front cover

THE FLATCOAT FABLES

GORDON G HALL

Prologue

The Flatcoat Fables are a short series of stories relating to a particular breed of dog. In many of the tales Flatcoated Retrievers are 'compared' with Labrador Retrievers and Golden Retrievers, and I have tried to capture the characteristics of each of these breeds, often relating them to their human counterparts.

The Fables are lighthearted pieces that, in what I hope is a gentle way, explain some of the quirkier aspects of the character of this wonderful breed. I have owned three Flatcoats - Saga, Folly and Epic, and whilst they were all very different characters they all exhibited at least some of the traits described in these stories. I hope that you enjoy them. If you own a Flatcoat you will understand what inspired them, if not then you have missed out on one of life's stranger and most rewarding of experiences!

I am indebted to Rieko Mamaoto for her charming illustrations, and to Nikita Ogurtsov for his great cover design

The Logs' are really meant for junior readers, although adults might be amused by them. They trace the developing relationship between two Flatcoated Retrievers being a series of internal conversations within the minds of the dogs.

At the turn of the century I owned two Flatcoats. Saga had been around for just over four years .. when along came Folly. These purported Flatcoat diaries are the reactions of each dog to this event. In order to distinguish between the two protagonists Saga's pieces are in a regular font, Folly's are in italic

I have tried to keep it true to the way that dogs think, that is they live 'in the moment' whilst such 'memory' as they possess is probably engendered by familiar things, especially scent. But this is not serious writing - please just enjoy it for what it is!

PART ONE

The Fables

1

Just So

Now where should we start? Perhaps at an early time when there were no Flatcoats, no Goldens, no Labradors, just a mish-mash of latent retrieving talent spawning in mist-wreathed kennel blocks in the heart of Victorian England.

Week Two [c.1870]

Listen very carefully and perhaps you can just make out the murmurings of a small litter –

"Who are we? "

"What will we look like when we grow up?"

"What are we going to do with our lives?"

"Where did that teat take itself?"

Just the everyday sort of puppy-talk that all retrievers wrestle with - but already differences seem to be developing between the three pups.

Week Eight [c.1890]

Puppy One has a slightly militaristic bearing. He bunches up his muscles and has already started to shave his coat which he secretly bleaches to a sort of yellowish colour.

Puppy Two has a rather more relaxed manner and a heavier gait. Although he cannot be bothered with all this shaving he has recently 'borrowed' some of One's bleach - not quite enough, so his coat is going a sort of rich gold colour.

Puppy Three just likes being a puppy and stays black!

Month Six [c.1920]

One is seriously out to impress. He knows just where he is going and is already busy networking with other kennels.

Two is nothing like so competitive, indeed he is rather embarrassed at One being so pushy, he clearly wants to please as many people as possible.

Three is still enjoying being a puppy – and stays black!

Year One [c.1940]

One already knows all the best shoots around the country and has invitations to most. He is moving into politics espousing a firm belief in popularism. His coat is now a fully formed 'short back and sides' and intrinsically yellow. Just occasionally he will dye it black so that he can be seen to be 'of the lads' .

Two is just the sort of fellow that you know you can rely on, dependable, honest, not very bright, but a really good chum. He wouldn't dream of dyeing his hair black.

Three occasionally wonders if she should stop being a puppy – but then thinks better of it. She stays black.

Year Three [c.1950]

One has sired a couple of litters that have all turned out the spitting image of him. Politics gave him a good start - everyone knows him - and he is now chairman of a rather dreary industrial firm. Although he occasionally gets out to the country he is very much town-based these days.

Two is already putting on a bit of weight, he is a clubbable sort of a chap and everyone likes him, both in town and at his place in the country.

Three does not seem to want to grow up - there is talk of psychiatry - her litter were all black, but when fooling around with her pups she squirted a bottle of washing up liquid over one of them and it has gone a sort of liver colour.

Year Ten [c.1980]

One has 'sired more litters than a rampant tom cat', aggressively he pumps iron every day. He has 'attitude'.

Two is suffering from gout (or arthritis) but is still really pleased to see you (sorry can't get up old boy). He has a large and rather scattered family who like to visit him at Christmas - but he has terrible trouble remembering all their names.

Three still behaves like a puppy, the occasional grey hair can be seen in her black coat - but what the hell - now how can I keep you all happy today!

Well, Oh Best Beloved (as the book goes), that is how the Labradors, the Goldens and the Flat-Coated Retrievers were made and how they developed. In contemporary human terms it is easy to recognise each breed: Labradors use mobile phones, Goldens will always buy you a pint of beer in a pub, and Flatcoats are forever young at heart and happy by nature.

2

Twas Ever Thus

Now whilst we are all entirely clear about the general development of the three Retriever breeds of Labrador, Golden and Flatcoat I have been taken to task for failing to explain 'The Quest' - by which is meant the trauma that our three developing puppies experienced as the character of their breed was truly established.

Although the exact moment it happened is lost in the mists of time I rather think that it was shortly before the 6 Month (1920) ! stage. Our three puppies had spent the day romping around, as young folk will, when their dam, the universal mother of our breeds, called them to her.

"There comes a time", she said, "When you have to seek your own way in the world. It is a harsh place, and getting worse by the year (and MacDonalds hadn't even been invented then!) and you will need Courage and Forbearance and Loyalty to sustain you, but you will also need that Special Something that makes you the dog that you really are. This Special Something is already within you, but to find it you will need to travel far and suffer much - you, my puppies, must undertake the 'Quest'."

So, the Lab Pup packed his map and compass, and the Golden Pup packed his oldest bone and his newest pillow and the Flatcoat Pup found her most bouncy tennis ball and off they went into the great Wide Blue Yonder. At the foot of the Great Mountains they came upon the kennel of Wise Old Hound. "You must cross the highest peaks," he growled, "and travel through the territories of the wildest wolves. You must swim the fiercest torrents, and all this will be easy - but you must also meet Man, and that is the sternest test of all for Man is more daunting than the peaks, more ravenous than the wolves and more destructive than the fastest river

Well, for many weeks they travelled. Lab Pup navigated them all the way with great care and great skill through unmapped mountains and unexplored valleys. Golden Pup parlayed with the Wicked Wolves charming them with his easy wit and honest manner so that they allowed the three pups to pass through their lands. And all the while Flatcoat Pup ran back and forth encouraging her companions in times of trouble, amusing them in times of depression and fearlessly swimming the rushing mighty waters (all the while holding her tennis ball).

The three became the greatest of friends and they all developed Courage and Forbearance and Loyalty. So at last they came upon the soft lush meadows, the quiet-flowing rivers and the villages of Man.

Man welcomed the pups into his houses and amongst his children and there they stayed for one whole lunar month.

Lab Pup told Man-children the story of their adventures and he showed them how to find their way safely from place to place and he was a popular pup!

Golden Pup let the Man-children ride on his back and he let the Man-babies pull his tail, and he was the friendliest of pups.

And Flatcoat Pup did back somersaults and carried three tennis balls in her mouth and rolled upside down with the Man-children in the hay-grass - and she was the happiest of pups

At the fullness of the moon the three pups were summoned before the Wisest Hound. "Pups," he said, "you have all developed Courage and Forbearance and Loyalty and that is how it should be from All Dogs, but you are Special Breeds and have each found that Special Something that makes Man want you in his houses and in his village.

"Lab Pup," said the Wisest Hound "You have done well, I grant you the attribute of Universal Popularity, you will for all time be a popular breed". And Lab Pup looked very important and pushed out his barrel chest and stuck his tail a little further in the air - and ever after was universally popular.

"Golden Pup," said the Wisest Hound, "You are the kindest of pups and I grant you the gift of Absolute Friendliness, everyone will forever be your friend." And Golden Pup put his heavy head between his paws and wagged his bushy tail and was from that day on always everybody's friend.

"Flatcoat Pup," said the Wisest Hound, and there was perhaps a twinkle in his rheumy old eyes, "you are a looney pup, to you I offer Eternal Happiness, from now on you will make everyone you meet as happy as you are!" And Flatcoat pup leapt three feet up in the air and caught a passing tennis ball, and Flatcoat Pup did three back somersaults running, and Flatcoat Pup smiled that special Flatcoat Smile that only Flatcoats smile - and she was forever Happy.

So, oh long-suffering reader, as your Flatcoat smiles at you and as you, of course, smile back you now know why you feel so happy!

3

Where the Spirit Moves

There comes a time in the development of any individual when there arises a very natural curiosity about Death and the Hereafter.

Following their return to the 'pack' after their first Quest our three, now near-adult, pups spent their time running and chasing and rolling and feeding and generally being Proper Retrievers. On the second month after their return however a rather more sombre mood descended upon them and their kin for every dog knew that Old Crusader, leader of the Retrievers was nearing the end of his life.

Crusader however insisted on maintaining his evening perambulation - meeting and greeting every member of the Pack - but on the Friday evening round he was clearly failing as he growled a kind word to the youngest of his family and climbed wearily onto his bench. For a moment he sat there, and then threw his heavy head up towards the heavens and, howling a great long defiant howl of departure, he died.

"What has happened to Crusader?"

"Why doesn't he move?"

"Has he gone somewhere else?"

The three pups were worried and curious and asked all the awkward kind of questions that their mother, the great Dam of all our Retriever breeds, found so difficult to answer. "You must go again and talk to the Wise Old Hound, Merlin," she told them, "but I am not sure that even he can give you an answer to all your questions"

So off went Lab Pup and Gold Pup and Flat Pup to see Merlin.

"Pups", said Merlin. "I can tell you that Death comes to us All. I can tell you that we have no more use for our bodies when we die, and I can tell you that the Memory of a great dog like Crusader lingers on for generation after generation. But as for the Spirit, that is something that you will have to discover for yourselves, an understanding of such things is part of that which makes you a mature and responsible Adult Dog. I have to tell you though that for this new Quest you must go your different ways, for some things have to be wrestled with on your own and by yourselves"

So the Three Pups chewed each other round the neck and tweaked each others' tails and said a cheerful goodbye to each other and set forth in different directions to find the Spirit of their Breed.

Lab Pup planned his expedition most thoroughly. He bought many atlases, several compasses, a sextant and the very best quad of walking boots that money could buy. He determined to cover the whole of the Known World in the most efficient and effective manner, So he climbed every line of longitude and slithered along every line of latitude. He trotted in the sunlight and he prowled at night. He met Capricorn and Cancer and he navigated scrupulously so as to cover the whole globe . . . .

Gold Pup was rather less energetic but he too had a Plan. He reasoned that The Spirit must be in the Elements, so he dug great holes around the (rather more civilized you understand!) parts of the world searching the Earth. He could be seen paddling for hours in the (fairly temperate you understand!) seas, searching the Waters. He spent a lot of his time sitting with his eyes half closed (in the interests of better concentration you understand!) sniffing the wind, searching the Air, but most of all he spent his time sprawled out (better to conduct this painstaking research you understand!) in front of as many warm hearths as he could find, searching Fire . . .

Flat Pup was not quite sure what a Plan was, she wondered if a couple of Tennis Balls would do instead? Anyway she set off in a generally Northerly direction and she skipped and she hopped and she grinned and she played. She waved to her friends, and she waved to strangers, she rolled on her back and she played tag and she was generally a very Irresponsible Flatcoat. And all the while her journeyings took her further and further to the North . .

Now Merlin was a Very Wise old hound and he knew that the pups would never come back to him with their answers to the Question, because he knew that this side of Death there is no answer, but he knew too that in their own way each of the pups would find the Spirit of their Breed.

Lab Pup did indeed cover the whole of the Globe. And he found in himself the Lab Spirit that was in the Yellow sunlight and in the Black shadows. It was in both the moonlight and the night and it was everywhere, planning, quartering, marching for ever.

Gold Pup searched Earth and Water and Air and Fire, and he found that the Spirit of Gold can be smelled in the freshly dug ground, seen in the rivers and lakes, heard as the leaves rustle in the wind, and felt by us as we huddle around the fire at night

Flat Pup went North until she could go no further. And there in the far North, she found the Flatcoat Spirit that dances and frolics, ducks and weaves and rolls on its back. It erupts in great flashes of colour and fun, subsides in joy and then rushes up again in great fountains of pleasure. So if we go out on a dark night and look towards the Northern Sky we can see there the Spirit of all the Flatcoats that have ever lived - playing together, pups forever - as the Northern Lights.

4

A Christmas Tail

Miss Suki Charmain Rooge was a most respected and re-spectable breeder of Flatcoated Retrievers, indeed she had been just that for most of her long working life. There was not a Championship that she had not won with her much sought after lines of dogs and not a country where Flatcoats are known which she had not graced with her sharp eye as a Judge of the Breed. She had served on the many committees and sub-committees of the Society and was now in the hon-oured position of either Vice-President or Patron of at least three International Breed Clubs. To sum up S.C Rooge was THE authority on Flatcoats - and she knew it!

Although it was Christmas Eve Miss Rooge was not going to be disturbed from her 'work' by any untoward festivity, indeed she blessed her good fortune to find herself quite alone that evening as she settled down to work out a most intricate arrangement of bloodlines that just might prove illuminating regarding an antipodean breeding of uncertain lineage.

An evening passed in such a manner tends to dull awareness of a heavy fall of snow and rising wind and so when the lights at first flickered, and then expired, Miss Rooge noted with some surprise what a wild night it was to have a power cut. Nothing daunted however she arranged a couple of candles and a Tilley Lamp and, for a while continued with her research, until an overwhelming tiredness seemed to consume her.

The shooting seemed remarkably close, just over the Blackthorne hedge. Miss Rooge peered through the thick brake to try to catch a glimpse of what was going on, and as she did so she was aware of a Flatcoated Retriever by her side, also poking its nose through the thorns. But WHAT a Flatcoat. Clearly he had had a day in the Field as he was caked with mud and his long straggly feathers were matted and tangled. He was not a very good specimen either thought Miss Rooge, running a professional eye over a rather too pronounced stop and a tail carried much too high.

"Hello!", said the Flatcoat.

Miss Rooge did not, for some reason find the idea of a conversation with this dog at all extraordinary, "Hello", she said," and who are you?

"I am the Ghost of Flatcoats Past", replied the muddy looking phantom wagging his tail in a very friendly manner and making to put his muddy front paws on her ample chest.

Miss Rooge said "DOWN",very firmly and looked at him archly. No Flatcoat had dared to take such liberties with her for many a long year, indeed as the author of 'Firm Flatcoat Training' she her reputation to consider!

The Ghost took the reprimand in good part and the two of them struggled through the hedge emerging just to the left of the shooting party. Miss Rooge noted the Plus Twos and the Norfolk Jackets and wondered why she should, amongst everything else that was happening to her, be subjected to Edwardian fancy dress.

Her companion must have guessed her thoughts, "No", he said, "it really is 1908 and as you can see the Breed is very much in vogue. We are the Best Gundog Breed by far and as you can see from my fellow flatcoats out here we are fit, healthy and, I can assure you, diseases such as cancer just do not exist within the breed"

"Oh", said Miss Rooge ,"but what a rag, tag and bobtail lot you all are. Why I wouldn't let any of you in the Society, let alone into any show ring that I was in charge of". Ghost shrugged his rather over-large shoulders, smiled an ethereal flatcoat smile, and vanished!

Miss S.C. Rooge was pleased to find herself back on home territory although a little surprised to discover herself out in her architect designed and scrupulously maintained kennels on what appeared to be a perfect summers day. Actually something seemed a little odd. she must be kneeling down because the iron railings seemed higher than usual. She stood up and rested her hands on the railings - only to discover that her arms were covered in black fur! She looked round - only to bang her long black nose on a brick pillar. "Ouch", she said - although it sounded more like 'squeak'!

"Steady", said a voice. "I know it takes a bit of getting used to - but you will soon get the hang of it". A friendly black muzzle shoved itself into her right ear and snorted at her. "I am the Ghost of Flatcoats Present", her new companion said, " I have to take you on a journey across a Great Ocean to see what is happening in the New World at this very moment". Almost before she realised it Miss Rooge and her friend were whisked into the air and set down in a foreign country.

There were Flatcoats everywhere, all prancing and dancing and dandering up their (rather short) feathers. Clearly they had arrived at the Specialty. "No", said her travelling friend, "we are not here to look at the dogs - just listen to what the Humans are saying".

" . . . no darn good at all, I quite agree, why how DARE such a person own one of OUR breed, why it will become quite COMMON if we let this sort of thing go on . . . ".

" . . . well, my dear, it's the COE, I mean did you ever HEAR of such a thing, if you ask me it's hereditary so we will have to neuter the whole litter . . . ".

" . . . yes, sooooo cute, all dressed up in a Snowman outfit and pulling a little sleigh with bells on . . ."

" . . . of course I have to shut him up in his crate when we are not there or he would swing from the chandeliers, but at night he is just super-cuddly under the duvet . . . "

Miss Rooge saw the scene fade slowly as she felt herself being dashed back home again. She looked one last time at the gentle face of Flatcoat Present and thought she had never seen such a wistful expression .. and was that just the start of a tear rolling out of the corner of an eye . . .

She was a little shocked at the appearance of the third Ghost. Beside her now stood the most perfect Flatcoated Retriever that she had ever even dreamed of. From its streamlined Borzoi head to its beautifully shaped hocks it was everything Miss Rooge had ever aspired to with her breeding.

"Of course you expected me," he said, "I am the Ghost of Flatcoats Future"

"But you are so perfect", said Miss Rooge in a manner close to adoration. "All my life I have tried to breed a dog as beautiful as you".

The ghoul looked as modest as a ghoul can. "Come", he said, and they were immediately looking down across half the shoots in England - and not a Flatcoat to be seen. Miss Rooge pondered, "These are all Labs and Goldies, she said. Show me some Flatcoats".

Again they were looking down, not at the wide open countryside now with its fresh air and healthy exercise, but at a series of funny little concrete squares in the centre of towns. "There you are";, said Flatcoat Future, "Flyball Parks - that's what we do now"

"Oh!", said Miss Rooge, "But what of the Show Ring, surely Flatcoats must be taking Best of Show now - that is if they all look like you".

"You won't like it", said her companion, but already they were in the midst of the judging. Miss Rooge thought she was in heaven, she had never seen such Flatcoated Perfection. She felt enthusiastic and excited about the future of the Breed, never mind that they no longer worked in the Field, here in the ring they were The Best.

She thought it a little odd that her fellow judge and she were in a chain-link enclosure, but rising, as ever, to the occasion she opened the barred gate and walked boldly into the ring better to discharge her duties as a respected Judge. Without hesitation fifteen snarling black (and two liver) brutes hurled themselves at her, jaws gaping, paws clawing at her. . there was slobber, blood, flesh . . and then calm as she rose up and away and away and away - and a ghostly whisper from her beautiful, perfect companion "It's the Temperament you see, they forgot the Temperament. . .

Miss Scrooge opened her eyes as the lights blazed on again. She got up very slowly and walked to the window. The snow had stopped falling and the wind had dropped. For a long time she stared out into the night. In her mind's eye she saw all the flatcoats she had ever bred and she assessed them all once again. Slowly she nodded. She walked back to her desk. She picked up the COE, she picked up the Breed Standard, she picked up her life's work on pedigrees and very deliberately she pushed them into the glowing embers of the log fire. Then she went outside.

She walked across to the kennel run and greeted each dog as it came to nuzzle her. "Flatcoats",,she said, and there was a new strength to her voice now, "I have made many mistakes, but from now on we start afresh. I will welcome the opinions of owners who are not breeders, I will breed for all-round ability and not for show, I will never rush to judgement about fellow Society members, I will never debase and denigrate my dogs, and, above all, I will learn again to love you all not for what I can make of YOU, but for what you can make of ME

And then it really was Christmas Day!

The Origins of Tennis

There is a certain misguided school of thought that considers the game of lawn tennis to have been developed in the last century from that of Court or Real tennis. This is quite untrue. The game was actually developed in order to ensure the proper evolution of the Flat-Coated Retriever.

Whilst a beautiful flowing black coat and a rather snipey muzzle were relatively easy to breed for, from existing Retriever stock, the first developers of the breed were determined to ensure that an innate desire to perform extraordinary retrieving and juggling feats should be an essential characteristic of the breed.

Therefore, in a somewhat clandestine fashion, many of the owners of the great English Country Houses began to set aside rectangular sections of their lawns so that they could try out a variety of 'retrieving aids'. Many 'retrieving aids' were invented, each developer claiming to have 'the best' .

In order to carry out objective trials it was decreed that white lines should be painted around the retrieving area and an agility obstacle (in the form of a long net) should be placed across it. Many were the House Parties devoted to the trials of 'retrieving aids' until a clear overall winner emerged in the form of a sort of yellowish soft furry ball. This seemed - and indeed has since proved - to be ideal for the recently created breed.

At this stage a schism occurred. True devotees of the new 'tennis ball' as it was called worked their Flatties with it and developed their expertise to such a pitch that no Flat-coat would ever be seen without at least one in a handy nearby spot (indeed my muse, Saga, liked to carry three in her mouth at the same time).

Sadly, some of the less sophisticated of those who had tested the retrieving aids adopted the new tennis ball as a sort of icon around which they developed a whole sporting industry - incidentally allowing use to be made of a redundant piece of real estate in the Wimbledon area.

The one thing that the early testers did find (and this is the mcral of this tale] was that with a yellow ball it was necessary to have a black dog - it being so much harder in retrieval trials to discern the exact moment when a yellow dog recovers a yellow ball! Therefore from that day forward yellow in a flatcoat has been banned from the breed standard.

6

Flat Relativity

There exists a serious misconception amongst the scientific community that Albert Einstein's theories of Special Relativity and General Relativity were original work and that subsequent physicists, such as Stephen Hawkin, developed from these theories further ground-breaking hypotheses such as those expounding Black Holes and Quantum Mechanics.

This is seriously wrong! The theory of Flat Relativity has existed since the Flatcoat was first developed.

Take Special Relativity first:

The idea that every individual carries their own 'clock' around with them - leading to the notion that the faster an individual travels the slower their 'clock' runs in relation to a stationary Observer is something that every Flatcoat learns at its mother's teat! Of course you have an internal 'clock' and the more you rush around at food-time, checking your bowl, dashing back to your Master, whizzing round in small circles, then the slower that beastly internal clock goes slower, and . . slower . . . . and . . s . l . o . w . e . r . . . . .

On the other hand if you just let it all hang out. . . shoot the breeze with a passing chum . . go with the flow . . snooze a little . . . . be yourself . . then your 'clock' runs faster and faster and it is mealtime before you can say 'shovel-it-into-my-bowl'. Quod est demonstrandum.

Now what about General Relativity do I hear you ask?

Unbelievably the same mistake was made and Albert got lauded for something that every Flatcoat has known about since the middle of the last century. Einstein postulated that Space/Time could be 'bent' by Mass - and this is the force that we call gravity. From the very first Flatcoat the Breed has been aware that the larger the Mass of food before it the more a Flatcoat's stomach will expand (even to infinity) to provide the Space required to accommodate it. Furthermore the faster a Flatcoat eats the slower

Time will run until eventually Time will stand still - until it has gobbled up the very last mouthful.

The Space/Time/Stomach Continuum is just basic common sense to the Flatcoat. Indeed if we take the theory a little further we can see that Eating is equal to the Mass of the food multiplied by the speed that it is eaten (normally at the speed of light squared - or C2), or as that latter-day plagiarist Albert Einstein sought to describe the eating habits of a Flatcoat: E = MC2.

So much for Einstein's theories, but what of more recent developments?

Clearly 'Black Holes' are just a description of the genuine Flatcoat (there are even a few Liver Holes!). Just in case some of our readers are not entirely clear about the properties of a Black Hole may I remind them that it is an object of almost unbelievable density from which no substance can escape once it is taken in. Somewhere at the centre of a Black Hole is a Singularity where the laws of physics are irrelevant and Time does not exist - need I say more?

Quantum Mechanics is a branch of physics, baffling to many humans, but all too familiar to Flatcoats. Indeed it is Flatcoat behaviour that actually identified this whole important field. QM is about discrete packages or 'particles' but it cannot make ts mind up as to whether they are on fact particulate or waveform. Flatcoats are uniquely qualified to know that this is due to the 'feathering' effect. Sometimes a Flatcoat can look like a discrete particle , and at others more like a wave (indeed we think that the individual feathers might even be important in String Theory.

Quantum Mechanics has it that although it is possible to say where a particle has just been it is only possible to make an informed guess where it might go, thus introducing unpredictability (this will sound very familiar to Flatcoat owners), further - the more energy you put into finding out where that 'particle' is at any one moment the more you disturb it and thus make it behave in an even more random manner (still sound familiar?)

7

Fireflies & Thistledown

As the three friends grew older they began to go their own ways, this did not diminish their love for each other, but, just as we humans need a little space of our own, each one of them discovered that as an individual they needed time to develop their own personality.

The Labrador youth discovered that some of his very best moments came from pushing himself to the very limit of his physical ability. He really enjoyed being stretched by his 'human' and doing absolutely everything that he was told - but in double-quick time!

Rather to the contrary his colleague the Golden Retriever found that his affability and innate charm were his biggest assets. He would hang around for hours (preferably by a good log fire) just to thump his tail and open wide his big brown eyes when his 'human' came in from work.

Flatcoat was just confused! She enjoyed working with Labrador, and even on a moderate day found she could out-run, out-sniff, and outwork him - but somehow she just could not see the 'deep and meaningful' in all this physical stuff. Neither was she slow to join Golden by the fire (indeed she tended to push in front 'ust to shield my friend from all that heat' but after an hour or two a certain sense of en-nui would pervade and she would turn her attention to the hearthrug ... or the log pile ... or the chair cushions (just to check that they are well enough made, you understand).

Labrador and Golden were concerned about their friend, She was the most gorgeous of companions, but seemed so 'disconnected', so unfocussed, so much of a flappity-gibbet! So . . Labrador planned the visit, organised the appointment, and packed the survival rations; Golden shoved a wad of the best pipe-tobacco in his pocket, pulled on his heaviest pair of plus fours, and left a note at his club to say that he was out of town for a day or two; and they both collected their friend Flatcoat and set off to see the Wizard Merlin.

Now in those days the woods in the Old Country were inhabited by witches, warlocks, hobgoblins and all manner of Petty Fiends - and of course the wise old hound Merlin lived in the deepest, dankest, darkest part of the very deep, dank, dark wood. By the end of the first day the three of them were very tired and not a little lost, what is more the dusk was gathering.

"We must make camp", said Labrador, and immediately set about trying to find a suitable site.

Golden sat down on a fallen tree trunk, pulled out his Meerschaum and started to tell a long, involved tale (to anyone who happened to be listening) about a chum of a chum of his who had once lost his way in up-country Malay - beyond the Cameron Highlands . . .

Flatcoat set off in chase of a firefly.

Whether it was Merlin, or some other Wizard, it is difficult to say, but as the gloaming turned to night a mist of smells rolled over that part of the wood and, just as human-kind get disorientated in a fog, our three heroes became befuddled and bemused in this cacophony of scent. At his best in a crisis Labrador carefully rolled out his sleeping rug, stowed his survival rations out of the way of crawling things, shut his eyes and went to sleep. Golden, unfazed by the whole thing, propped himself up against his tree trunk, pulled his cape a little closer around his ample form, took a (purely medicinal) slug of Brandy and Soda from his hip flask, and went to sleep.

Flatcoat danced on and on after her fireflies, leaping higher and higher, further and further, lighter and lighter . . . until her semi-conscious mind was a blur of rhythm and scent and pleasure. And in this dream-trance she saw a great shimmering curtain of raw, naked light. And in the centre of this Light she could dimly discern a Great Presence. She felt herself drifting towards this Thing of Power, feeling nothing but Peace.... she was surrounded by words whose meaning she couldn't grasp, by scents she had never smelt and by sounds of whose origin she could not guess. For an age she seemed caught up in this maelstrom of experiences and then she heard a far off Great Voice intoning "It Is Done! Go My Flatcoat, Go In Peace". . . and she was standing on the damp floor of the Forest howling a great howl of longing and love, howling to the trees and the sky and the stars, howling to her friends, and their friends and all the friends in the whole Wide World.

Labrador and Golden woke instantly to find the scent-fog had gone. They both rushed to the sound of their friend who was now standing, spooked, in a small clearing in the wood. "What happened", they cried, overjoyed to find her alive and well, "where have you been

Flatcoat said nothing

They left the wood and retraced their steps, until eventually they arrived back home. There seemed however to be even more spring in Flatcoat's step than usual, and was it just imagination or did the youthful twinkle that had always been in her eye, not shine just a little brighter now?

A few weeks later they were sitting in the sun in the kennel yard. "It seems to me", said Golden, "that, like Dorian Grey, we have, in the end, to pay for our attributes. Take you, my friend Labrador, your persistence and assertiveness can, on occasion, just tiptoe into aggression can it not"

Labrador gave a (fairly) friendly growl of assent, "And you, Golden old mate, your docility and decency can become rather over-chummy, and (not that I mind of course) that can be a little overwhelming if coupled with just a hint of body-odour."

Golden looked a bit startled, sniffed a bit of anatomy, and grunted something by way of assent. "But what about you, Flatcoat. Surely you have never been happier than these last weeks. It seems that you have been granted the gift of Pertpetual Youth? You will dance and prance and sing your way through life without a care and without seeming to age a day in a whole year! There must be something you have to pay in recompense for this?"

And Flatcoat smiled at her friends. Flatcoat smiled a peculiarly Flatcoat Smile. Flatcoat thought of the Great Presence and how she had seen all the Good Things she could do with the Everlasting Youth that she had been granted, but she also saw again what she had seen that night, she saw the Cancer that was to bedevil her breed, she saw the suffering and the sorrow that this would bring both to Flatcoats and their Humankind, and she saw again the Dreadful Choice that she had been asked to make. And she thought again, and knew that even if she had the chance once more, she would make that same Choice. Yes, the pleasure and happiness and sheer joy she could give to all around her throughout her allotted span would be worth the sorrow and the pain that the End would inevitably bring. Yes, she smiled, she had chosen well . . .

"Oh, Come on," she said, "Come on you two stuffy old things. Let's go chase thistledown across the meadow. . . . .'

PART TWO

The Logs

8

﹉

LOG ONE

In which Saga discovers that Dog Shows
are not places to sell disgraced Flatcoats
and certain suspicions start to trouble her.

Today (Isn't it Always)

There is something: AFOOT!
What is going on?
Several Today's Ago we go to a thing called Dogshow
Masters talking to other Masters with several ME
Lots of ME all walking with Masters looking
Never seen anything like it
Meet friendly Me called Maddy
Maddy says dogshow is for selling
Help! I am going to be sold!
I KNEW Gordon was upset about Deer Slot thing

I never thought he sell ME!
Hey, that was a real Something Smell ......Oooh!
I am NOT sold! Whew .. that was close

Still Today - (isn't it always!)
Several Today's Ago went to two House of Dogs
Masters come out smelling Very Interesting Indeed
What does the word 'Puppy' mean?
I know its something good - it makes me roll on back
Lots of things make me roll on my back . . .
. . . like scratchy behind the shoulders..... Oooh! ....

Still Today - (isn't it always!)
...and another thing!
I know my bed Today Ago is a bit small
Bed very good for curly from cold in Winter
Well Today Gordon saws it in half
Yes, honestly.. with a saw!
I watch him VERY CAREFULLY
What is he up to NOW?
Would you believe it, he puts it together again !
My bed is bigger now - GREAT
I stretch out on my super-bed and hang loose . . .
Gordon shakes his head and scratches my ear
Gordonsez bed is still a bit small
Funny. . . it has done me for Umpteen Today's Ago
Never mind, just stretch that back leg out ....Oooh
....

Still Today - (isn't it always?)
There is something called Five Weeks Old
There is something about telling ME
'This Will Put Your Long Black Nose Out Of Joint'
I am a very confused Me
Is anyone able to help ME ?
Hey, a tennis Ball - no time to chatter . . .. Oooh! . ....

Me - Saga

9

LOG TWO

In which Saga thinks she is seeing double,
the word 'puppy' is mentioned again,
and honour is satisfied in relation to Cats.

Today (Isn't it Always)
Hello again, yes it's ME!
The plot THICKENS
What is Gordon up to?
Today Day Ago (or Ago Ago) he started wiring gates
Yes, every gate in the garden.
Not that he is very good at it ...
... I try to tell him visiting cats can get through
He mumbles something about not-get-through
Even small SEVEN-AND-A-HALF-WEEKS
WHAT is week?

I am an even more confused ME!
Now I buried that bone somewhere ... Oooh! . . .

Today (isn't it always!)
. . . . and what about this Beanbag thing?
I know that was being rough with old beanbag
Today Ago, Masters bought TWO new ones
And some more feeding bowls. .
Clearly I am going to get double rations !!!!!!
Life is looking up - Masters CARE ABOUT ME
I am a VERY IMPORTANT ME
I have:
Very Large Bed,
Two Beanbags and
Four Feeding Bowls.
Now if you could just scratch behind my right ear ...
. . . just a little higher please.. Ooooh! . . . .

Today (isn't it always!)
Today Ago we visit House of Dogs again
What is 'Six Weeks Old Today'?
Gordon goes all sort of gooey and strange
I sit in Alfacar and pretend I cannot smell anythin
BUT I sniff a sniff that reminds ME of something
Something I knew Today Ago and Ago and Ago
so far Ago that it is hardly proper Today ... .
This is a Good Sniff... ...j
Just curl front upper lip and sniff deep ...Oooh!

Same Today (isn't it always!)

When leaving House of Dogs
Gordon lets ME out of Alfacar for pee
 Start pee - - - see CAT - - - - Whoooooosh
Gordon YELLS at ME
CAT runs up tree ME YELLS at CAT
Woman owning House of Dogs laughs
She say ME a Proper Flatcoat
I do nonchalant pee and step graciously into Alfacar
I like House of Dogs
Nothing bad can ever come from House of Dogs
Now stretch on leather seat ... Ooooh!

Today (isn't it always!)

Snooze time now
In dreams says "week on Tuesday for Puppy."
Me twitch
Me has called to mind 'puppy'
In dreams .. I sniff puppy sniff..
ME is puppy - (squeak)
In dreams .. everyone gooey over ME - (thump tail)
In dreams.. nearly .. understand - (twitch paws)
Snooze . . . . .
What a life.. nothing to disturb ME .. ever...
Snooze . . . . Oooh! . . .

Me - Saga

10

LOG THREE

In which Saga regrets the current situation

Today (wish to be Today Ago!)
Oh NO NO No!
Nobody told ME
********* HEY - WOW ******** Whassattt!
GRRRRR !
WHIZZZ ********
~******** YELP *******
I'll NEVER trust Gordon again - NEVER !
OUCH ! ! ! ! !
GRRRRR!

Me -
Saga

11

LOG FOUR

In which Saga is less than impressed
by Follything and her early upbringing,
whilst Folly explores Life In General

Today (Isn't it Always)
Me most unhappy ME
Today Ago Ago is Disaster Day
Today Ago is bad day for ME
ME life is ruined by this Follything
Best to totally ignore
So nowToday smells better
Hey is that a butterfly? - LEAP – Oooh

Today - Now
SagaSez GO AWAY
SagaSez I am a right little ME

> *I LOVE Saga*
> *Oooh -ish!*

Still Today - (isn't it always!)
> This Folly Thing always thinking ME its Dam
> This Folly Thing thinking ME a Milk Bar!
> This Folly Thing needs putting in its place - Grrr!
> Wow! Did you see that stick hit the water? - Oooh!

Today - Now
> *SagaSez Trot round the Garden*
> *SagaSez Collapse panting under chair*
> *SagaSez Sniff in this flower bed*
> *I LOVE Saga*
> *Oooh-ish!*

Still Today - (isn't it always!)
> I pick BIG BONE with FollyDam, called - 'Flirt'
> Flirt regurgitate food for small MEs
> This Folly Thing thinking me a canine cud chewer!
> This Folly Thing jumping, licking my mouth - Grrr!
> Today postman call twice - what a WOOF! - Oooh!

Today - Now
> *SagaSez this place called Vet*
> *SagaSez this Ouch Place . . .*
> *. . . . OUCH ! Saga Always Right!*
> *I LOVE Saga*
> *Gordon Thing says I will not get disease*

Gordon stupid
Ouch Needle makes ME dis - ease!
Time for Breakfast Squeak - Oooh-ish

Saga and Folly

12

LOG FIVE

In which Saga racks her braincell and protects
her wagging appendage whilst Folly explores
the niceties of Potentilla shrubs and birdbaths

Today (Isn't it Always)
Me am sure that Long Long Today Ago was different
Something is missing then - perhaps?
Is there ever a Today Ago without Follything?
Me racking Flatcoat Brain - nothing but Follything!
Aha - a shady Potentilla shrub to lie under - Oooh!<

Today - Now
SagaSez lie under Potentilla shrub . . .
I LOVE Saga
Lie under Potentilla shrub with Saga
SagaGrow - No Worry - pounce SagaTail *******

*****Hey! - Wow! - *****
Little ME downside-up in Black Maelstrom!

Still Today - (isn't it always!)
ME a bit touchy about tail
Gordon always laugh and says tail too feathery
Gordon says ShowDogs get tail trimmed
Me think maybe Follything try trimming!
Very Hot Day - BirdBath best place for ME - Oooh!

Today - Now
SagaSez lie in Birdbath
Splosh! - Wow - Better than upsetting waterbowl
Hi Saga - Look at ME - Splosh!
Saga go away rather quickly . . . .
Hi Gordon - look at ME - Splosh!
Ouch Gordon - That's Neckscruff!

Saga and Folly

13

LOG SIX

In which Saga rather reluctantly assumes a tutorial role, Folly eats Foul Things and is nearly returned to Breeder!

Today (Isn't it Always)

Today Ago Ago no FollyThing!

Trying to play with FollThing

It keeps jumping at mouth

ME trying to train IT

Mouth-jumping not A Good Thing for Sagas

Tail-pulling Worse!!! Grrrrr.. . . OOWF!

Hope Gordon takes me to work

Gordon passenger boat good - Rest Needed!

Aha - here comes FerryVan - bye . . . Ooooh. . .

TodayNow

> *SagaFriend keeps avoiding me*
> *I love SagaFriend*
> *I think SagaFriend got bad memory - forgets me here*
> *Saga Friend snoozy - Hey she got scraggy ear-hairs . . .*
> *OW - OW - OW -*
> *SagaBoss got snappy white front teeth !!*

Today (Isn't it Always!)

> Today Ago no FollyThingy
> Now just grab the other end of this bone . . .
> That's right now PULL
> Now FollyThingy
> This is where we lie down to keep cool . .
> NO NOT IN Hosters ! !There I tell you
> Whappings for Hoster destruction!
> NO Thingy - Don't eat THAT
> It just emerged from YOU!
> There you are - more whappings!
> Now Lunch Time - If I just look a little pathetic,
> a little bit &'butter-wouldn't melt' . . .
> . . . it worked! Ooooh . . . .

Today Now

> *Hey! me just a puppy . . .*
> *Hey! whappings are against Canine Rights*
> *I only eat it 'cos it smells good!*
> *Me NOT 'disgusting, filthy, foul, little urchin!'*
> *Me on't want 'postage stamp stuck on head*

With message: 'Return to Breeder'
. . . and Hosters are good for shadyplace.
SagaFriend sticking up for me
When SagaFriend WOOF me woooooof like her
me Great Help to SagaFriend . .

.

Today (Isn't it Always!)

Today Folly ME Friend!
ME lie on back and FollyFriend jump on ME
ME playfight with FollyFriend
Gordon stupid saying FollyFriend FourWeek stay
Never been a time without FollyFriend
FollyFriend, this is where CATS get into garden . . .
Yes, that's right, nose down, curl lip . . .
Wow it's hot - just off to the lake,
Come on FollyFriend . . .Ooooh . . . ..

TodayNow

SagaSez me her Friend
Oh WOW! - me SagaFriend !! me love Saga
. . .Very worried about Saga Saga shrinking!
Actually whole world shrinking
Even Gordon shrinking (so he should!)
How do I stop WorldShrink ???????
What does GROWING mean ?
Gordonsez me Growi Up. Perhaps that means more food .

Saga and Folly

14

LOG SEVEN

In which Saga gets wrongly blamed and tries some
conceptual thinking,whilst Folly goes on her
Very First Walk and meets Strange Things.

Today (Isn't it Always)
    FollyFriend is big today
    There is something called 'remember'
    ME has forgotten 'remember'.
    If ME could do this remember
     Perhaps ME would understand 'grow'?
    As it is ME know Follything is jumping around ME
    Me and Follything ush around kitchen
    And breakfast room bashing into chairs
    Gordon Yell at ME. This is not right -
    FollyThing bash chairs
    ME under OakTable where Gordon too fat to crawl

Lick paws, think Good Things - Oooh!

Today - *Now*

Me out of Purdah - Gordon say 'injections finished'
Today go for 'walk with SagaFriend
What is walk? Find out soon - SagaFriend knows 'walk'
SagaFriend leaps about and carries GordonWalkStick
Hey! Walk is Good - bouncing up old track behind garden
Cannot see over stone walls but find gate
HRRRROOOOPMPH!
WOW - WASSSATT!
Jump two feet in air off all paws and look again
Enormous Piebald Brute on other side of gate -
It went hrrrrooomphing at me!
This Walk Thing only good in parts!

Today - (isn't it always!)

FollyClot frightened of farm pony!
Now walks are for Good Sniff,
Come along FollyClot, nose down!
Here is a 'remember-scent' - Badger here in nightime
Next 'on-top' 'remember-scent' is Red Deer
Me think Deer coming to GrassMunch
Perhaps 'remember' does mean something
Like 'scent-below-last'
Gordon says this is 'conceptual thinking'
He say SagaBrain is too small
Gordon a bit weak in BrainCell department
He too stupid and cannot sniff Deer

Perhaps Gordon Brain too small for 'Sniff Think'
Now this is a really Foul Thing . . . . Oooooh.

Today - Now!
Tail Chop!
me VERY attached to furry end of tail
GordonMate picks me up - me thinks 'aha, PuppyCuddle'
Scissors flash, me wriggle, SNIP, end of tail fur gone!
This is Not Right.
Clearly time to empty a few wastebins
Me can shred a newspaper or two
Garden needs digging - Digging needs bringing into House
OUCH!
Where is the number for PuuppyLine - ME not vandal
ME never tried to cut THEIR fur off!

Saga and Folly

15

❧

LOG EIGHT

In which much is made about dog-beds and training

Today (Isn't it Always)
    Now ME think me tell you Today Ago about Bed?
    Well Gordon make SagaBed bigger
    I think 'Good, more room for SagaStretch'
    FollyThing thinks extra bedsize for her
    ME growl. SagaTail NOT for lie-on
    FollyThing has bed on floor - Good Place!
    GordonMate say 'Poor Folly with bed on cold floor'
    Gordon snarl a bit
    GordonMate and say Sagabed big enough for two
    GordonMate gives Gordon A LOOK
    Gordon dismembers Sagabed and make VERY BIG
    ME has 6 ft bed WOW!
    Stretch . . . yawn . . . ooooh

TodayNow

Sagabed is big now - too big for SagaFriend
me leap on Folly/Sagabed
Whoopeee! No SagaGrowl!!
Me sleep with Saga now - very-grown-up-puppy!
Gordon rude about me looks. Gordon call me 'sewer-rat'
Me sleek and lovely with long smooth tail and nosegrow
Gordon wrong!
me went on boat Today Ago with SagaFriend
Passenger say 'I like your dogs - especially the small one'
Whopeee - did you hear that?
ESPECIALLY THE SMALL ONE

Today (Isn't it Always?)

Gordonboats getting very poor quality of passengers

TodayNow

Me has found more about this thing called Walks
Walks are not just 'half an hour to Moss Eccles Tarn'
(me like Moss Eccles Tarn - Splosh!)
Walks can happen anytime, just collar-on and away!
 Best walks have Open Fell
Best walks have Lakes or Tarns
Best walks have Deersniff, Foxsniff and SquirrelSniff
Me has brain that works well on sniff
But brain disengages ears when noseworks
Gordon talks about thing called Training
Gordon say Training engage brain when nosesniff

Training might be fun
Training is SIT before foodtime
Training is STAY before romptime
Training is ON-THE-BOAT at jetty-docks
Gordon say 'Good Girl' and I get foodthing REWARD
Me like Reward. me like Training. me Proper Flatcoat!

Today (Isn't it Always?

FollyThing Talk too much - whose Log is this?
Anyway Me train Follything
Who show her Deersniff?
Who play swim-in-Tarn?
Who growl when Follything chews tableleg?
Who show her rubbish-bin?
Who show her upend-rubbish-bin?
Who help her chew best bits of rubbish
Who sneak off so only FollyThing gets Whapping?
Now that is Proper Training!!
Sardine cans, Camembert wrappers, Ice cream Tubs
Oooooh . . . . . !

Saga and Folly

16

LOG NINE

In which Saga worries about Folly's size -
and gets into BOTHER,whilst Folly is
Very Well Behaved - until she discovers Ice Cream

Today (Isn't it Always)
Worried about FollyGrow
Will this FollyThing ever stop getting bigger?
ME very kind and BedShare with her,
But BedShare is getting out of paw
ME allocate small corner of bed as FollySpace
Now SagaStretchSpace getting smaller and smaller
It's Gordon and GordonMate's fault
Too much FollyFeeding . . .
Now SagaFeeding, that's different . . . .
Yummmmm . . .just one more tasty morsel . . . . oooh!

TodayNow

me VERY GOOD PUPPY!
me go for Walk with SagaFriend
me do everything GordonSez . . BUT
SagaFriend NOT GOOD GIRL !!
SagaFriend find Deersniff and whoooosh! Gone!!!
Gordon whistle, me come back . . ,
me think Saga got Earblockage as she not hear.
Gordon growl a bit at Saga
All go through BullockField with Lots of Beasts!
me try to say "hello" to bullock.
Bullock says "Phrooof"at me and charges .me . .
HELP !!!!!
TAKE TO THE HILLS !!!
RUN FOR YOUR LIVES !!!
me right behind Gordon, he might need help with bullocks!
Saga shows she not concerned . . . .
. . .she VERY 'GUSTING eat BullockShit !!
Gordon YELLS at Saga - - - SagaSlink!
me looks cute and as if poo wouldn't melt in me mouth . . .

Today (Isn't it Always?)

Huh! So WonderPup does it again!
Who teaching FollyThing everything it knows?
Who putting up with Earbite every Today?
Who show FollyThing how to walk to heel?
Who defend FollyThing against Bullocks?
One little lapse from perfection . . . . . !
ME going to find new Gordon,

This Gordon VERY BAD NEWS
Just think:
A nice Gordon,
A kind Gordon,
A NoGrowl Gordon
. . . ooooh!

TodayNow

Me on Boat TodayAgo
Me find nice family of SmellyBrats
SmellyBrats have yummy sniffs called Icecream
Me look cute. SmellyBrats like cute.
Gordon doing JettyDockThing with spokeywheel
So Gordon not looking at what me is doing
Me just want to taste YummyCream . . . .
SLURRRRRP !
SmellyBrats YELL at me,
SmellyBrats Dam YELL at SmellyBrats
Gordon YELL at me
Gordon doing JettyDockThing VERY BADLY . .
Me complain Gordon incompetent to Marine Safety.
Gordon mutter about:
YardArms and
PlankWalks and
KeelHauls
for Flatcoats! Me not very nautical . . .
. . . me like yummy icecream though

Today(Isn't it Always?)

See what I mean . ..

Saga and Folly

17

LOG TEN

In which Saga gets 'girly' about her hair on her birthday,
whilst Folly ponders the meaning of Christmas -
and wonders what Gordon is going to do to her now.

Today (Isn't it Always)
  Bad Hair day today!
  Black locks all whichways and full of burrs
  Tried teeth-pull but mouthfullup of burrs
  Tail worst bit - very sraggley
  Not me fault, just FLATCOATING around village
  Chase Cat, dig garden, chase cat, empty birdbath,
  Never gets me anywhere -
  'But me wasn't sure me was going anywhere anyway!!
  Winter is museing-time really . .
  Me muse on Cats, and Bones, YELP!!! Let Me tell you

. . .

TERRIBLE THING IN ENGLAND-WORLD
Gordonsez 'Government' banned Marrow-Bones
Ban is because of BSE
Me not know who Government is
Me agree banning bones Bloody Stupid Exercise!
Now where did I bury that old one . . . Oooooh

TodayNow

THEY bring tree into house
Me in trouble when me bring small twig into house!
Great Big Tree - HUGE - and they not in trouble
Put funny things on tree - also chocolates !! YUM !!
Chocolates supposed to be for Twelfth Night
Methink Twelfth Night is NightNow
Me in lots of Lots of trouble-ouch!
Candle-lights all this Christmas-thing
Gordon mutters growly things about Electricity Board
Me think tail-wag good for candles - very splutter
SagaSez Christmas without Marrow-Bone is dismal,
But me wonder what Christmas is about
Could be just Chocolate and Candles and Marrow-bones,
or something else . . ? Me not thinkful enough to know

Today(Isn't it Always?)

Hey! Saga Birthday Today!
ME having Birthday - Twelfth night party
Gordon says I should be Malvolio
If so methink he be Sir To.....OUCH Gordon!
FollyThing is as big as Me now,but Me BossDog!

Anyway Follything Big Chicken
When Follything DoorWoof she sounds VERY fierce,
But when DoorKnock come she dash back to den
Then follow behind Me to SortOut!
Me know Gordon plans to unzip FollyThing
Saw Gordon go to Ouchey-Vet for Appointment
Follything not know what coming to her . . .
Now just scratch my back will you . . . . Ooooooh

TodayNow

What's 'Unzip' mean? methink something nasty
It lurks in very small thing called GordonMind
(must be small 'cos GordonNose is so tiny
A GordonMind is at end of Nose.
Lots of new things for Growing Teeny-Bopper
To enjoy and to to explore
Me woke up TodayAgo and grass had gone!
That's right, went to Follybed at night . . . .
. . . . In morning NO GRASS ! True!
Lots of cool white stuff very good to BOUNCE in
Me jump, me leap, me dodge SnowballThing,
Me chase in circles. Very Good Day
Wake up in morning grass is back.
Very strange - perhaps me dream?
Me still worried about 'Unzip'-
Gordon say UnzipDay is Monday
Hope they don't take me stuffing out . . .
. . . . . . .me like me stuffing !

Saga and Folly

18

LOG ELEVEN

In which Folly is spayed and discovers Haagen-Daz,
whilst Saga has a day on the boat
and ruminates on Veterinary Practices

TodayNow

> Terrible Thing happens to me TodayAgoAgo
> Me jumps in RattletrapVan with SagaFriend
> Gordon not go BoatWays
> M going to AmblesideVillage - Very Big City
> Me thinks "Yippee, yummy smellings"
> Gordon make SagaStay but says "FollyCome"-
> So me Van OutJump on leash.
> MeThinks Tough on Saga!
> Me cross Great Highway . . .
> . . . and go into Old Soldiers live house.
> No soldiers - just a ColliePup and a Cat-in-Cage.

Me Good, me SIT, me say HowDoYouDo to ColliePup,
Methink cat lucky no Saga . . .

Today (isn't it Always?)

Me not want to OutJump Van.
Me see FollyThing cross little one-way street
Me know Old Soldiers not live in place called 'Vets'
This is NewVet 'cos Gordon cross with OldVet
OldVet not MeFriend either
NoVet MeFriend
When Me Very Small Gordon take me Greg's school
me meet GordonFriend who is Vet longwaysaway
He say to G. "Ha! A Flatcoat!
Only one brain cell in whole breed"
Gordon Think VetFriend Very Funny.
Me upset!
Me do dump on Uppingham School Quad Lawn -
Me embarrass Gordon!
Ha! More to Flatcoat than one BrainCell !!!
Now FollyThing talking of Cat-in-Cage . . . .
Grrrrr, Yelp, Me want CAGEOPENER - Oooooh!

Still Today (isn't it Always!)

ME say to FollyThing "WatchOut, this UnZip Place"
ME knows 'cos OldVet UnZip ME
AnyHowWays Me have Good Day
ME help with antifouling Boats all red colour
ME thinks Me coat has small red-tinge problem!
Also lipstick 'cos me PickUpRetrieve StirStick

Gordon worried about ME Red Lips
Gordon muttering about Cellulose Thinners
ME do very crafty job
ME entice Ornamental Chinese Goose to lakeshore
Whooheyyy! SPLOSH!
GordonYell,
GooseYell,
ME stick nose in air. Pretend ME looking for fish!
Gordon cross 'cos ME VeryWet
But ME smack RedLips at him
ME give him BrownEye Look - Ooooooh!

TodayNow

Friendly VetNurse asks me to stand on WeighPad
Me weigh '26 kilos' Gordon say "What are kilos?"
Gordon old stick-in-mud.
VetMan come, rub me ears, say he like Flatcoats
VERY SNEAKY THING TO SAY
'Cos he NeedleJab me at same time!
We go and sit opposite Cat-in-Cage
ColliePup keels over and all DozyEyes . . .
VetNurse come in and I jump up and Tailwag
She say "Aren't you dozing off yet"
Gordon say I AM dozy
He sayshe should see me when I am not full of DozyStuff
VetNurse learning Flatcoats not same thing as CollieDogs
. . but I decide to sit down for a bit . .
. . GordonLeave Me very nice . . and warm . . and dozy . .

MightBe Today or NotSoNow

WhasattEverSoAwfulGiddyWhirleaboutHeadFeeling
Me on VetFloorRug AllOutStretchFloppy
DozyFeel HeadUp UghYuckSick HeadDownAgain
SmellGoneFunny.All GiddySniff . .
AllScentsWhirringRoundInKaleidascopeNose

. .

Today (Probably)Now

Me sniffout ColliePup. ColliePup in Cage
Me thinksAgo Cat-in-Cage
Very TopsyTurveyThink
Me like VetNurseGirl, just try to stop nosewhirl . . .

Today (isn't it Always!)

Me fed up going to AmblesideVillage
Could go for ForestWalk instead
ME see FloppyThing stagger across road
FloppyThing cannot BigLeap in VanBack
ME sniff FollyFriend VeryScareySmell
ME try ThinkBack WobblyLegs Feeling
Gordon drive Very Slow to HomeKennel
FloppyBundle left by fireside while ME FEED
Should have FollyFood too - Me eat for her . . .
Yummmmm Ooohhhh

TodayNow-ish

Me TummySore. Me had stuffing OutTaken!
Me very attached to stuffing - cruelty! - me snooze . . .

TodayAgain-ish

Me TailWag.

Me sniff Haagen-Daz. 'Special FollyTreat!

Perhaps me not so attached to stuffing!

TodayLater

Me go back to VetPlace and go in with SagaFriend

Me tailwag and lie on table

SagaFriend ShiverAndPant - dashes for WallOpenPlace

VetMan says me good at StitchesOut

Gordon says Saga Big Scaredy Custard

Saga not being StichesOuted

Me thinks more Haagen-Daz Treats needed . . .

Today (isn't it Always!)

ME think this is a Rotten Log!!!!!

ME think it is all about FollyThing and Vets

Me do RollOnBackWith PawsInAir

Hope some nice reader come and TickleTum . . . .

. . . . . . Oooooohhhhh!

Saga and Folly

19

LOG TWELVE

Further problems with sleeping arrangements,
Saga ruminates on Flatcoats not chasing tennis balls,
whilst Folly considers Flatcoats that do not swim.

Today (Isn't it Always)
Things not Good TodayAgoSomeTime
You remember how LongTodays Ago
Gordon makes SagaBed
Well, FollyThing convinced SagaBed is FollyBed
THIS NOT SO !!!
SagaBed is Inviolate (well sort of tan coloured really)
It is Saga Alone Place
All Flatcoats need AlonePlace to Cogitate!
ME Cogitate - Gordon say Cog is rusty - Grrrrrr!
AnyHowWays FollyThing jump on SagaBed
Gordon say "Good, Keep SagaWarm"

ME DISTRESSED
ME PANT and HAVE PALPITATIONS
ME not at all Oooooooooh

TodayNow

Yipee! SagaFollyBed FUN
Me LeapOn SagaFollyBed, now LeapOff, now LeapOn
Me chew SagaFollyRugOnBed nightimes,
Me pull RugCushions,BedBits all over floor
Me happy adolescent Flatcoat
Me FlattyBopper!
Gordon GrowlaBit
GordonMate GrowlaLot
Saga VeryFunny Old Stick In Mud!

Today - (isn't it always!)

GordonMate make new FollyBed
Made from old palletwood
ME go quickly to bed nightimes before Folly come in
ME stretch. NoseTip longwaysaway from TailTip
Folly not invade SagaSpace, go to new FollyDivanBed
ME HAPPY. Gordon call me cussed old B*******
ME not chew Lino or scratch walls
GordonMate say me Strange Dog!
Now just one more cushion, please . . . . .Ooooooooh!

TodayNow

Thing is that me want to stay Black
Me worried about turning red 'cos fluffy bits got RedTinge

Methink flatcoats get greyness todayahead
SO methink CoalChew is answer.
Me take coal out of brass coal scuttle (just Flatcoat height)
and Coal Munch on carpet, on rug, and on window seat . .
GordonMate behaving oddly . . .
GordonMate chase FlattyBopper round house growling!!
But me SEE GordonMate do coal thing in fireplace
She take coal out of scuttle,
Then in morningtime she take old coal out of grate
I good at takung take coal out of grate likewise
But me in Number One GordonMate Trouble!

Today - (isn't it always!)

This FollyThing not much of Retriever
Follything not chase Tennis Balls !!!!
What Flatcoat does not chase Tennis Balls ??
She retrieve everything else
Most particularly Yucky Things
Follything found really Yummy Sheep Dagging
She brought it onto GordonBoat
Gordon nearly stood on Yummy
Gordon CrazyMad at Follything
ME thought Folly get thrown Overboard!
But Yummy went over instead!
ALSO FollyThing not run much!
ME always run, and run, and run all walklong.
ME backlegs get cramped after longwalks,
Now just one more throw . . . . . Oooooooooh!

Today*Now*

What is all this with Tennis balls?
Now me tell you Big Secret (shhhhh) . . .
. . . SagaFriend scaredy-custard of swim !!!
Not that she can't swim ('cos me see her paddle)
Just that she make lots of antiswim excuses
Shesez Lost me Stick, seen a Friend, got to Scratch
Now me WaterBaby! Methink FollySwim well
Me leap in swim Tarn or swim Lake
Me even try to get in GordonBath
This not advisable, Gordon Big and Soapy!
Also very growly about sharing bath!
Anybody know about thing called Birthday ????
Sagasez me nearly ready for First Birthday
Me bit aprehensy-thing about this Birthday
Whassit? Is it Friendly? Does it Bite?
Please send advice marked 'ForFol'

Saga and Folly

LOG THIRTEEN

In which Saga wrestles with Time, the Universe,
Decent Behaviour and BSE, Folly finds her pedigree,
and discovers marrow bones and mooring warps

Today (Isn't it Always)
Now the Thing Is . . .
Well you see it is like this . . .
It's this Cogitate Thing
Sometimes Me 'Cogs' just do not cogitate properly
'Cos Me has a Big Unsolved Problem
How can Me explain . . .
If Me is here, and Moment Ago Me is there,
And Moment Next me is elsewhere . . .
Well WHAT is this Moment Thing?
WHAT is it Up To ? Me tries to smell Moment
But Moment has Very Elusive Sniff

Me even try poke FollyThing in ribs
So she Whizz Off PlayGameThing
But Moment must go with her like Shadow.
Me listen what Gordonsez
GordonSay genius Einstein think Good Moment.
Me think such things are not for Flatcoats,
Me wonder are there Things not for Humans
All a bit too much 'Cogi' for Me
Me lie on back and wave paws in air . . . Ooooooh!

TodayNow

Hey! Wow! Wow! Hey!
Wowowowowowowowowowowowowowo!!!
You gotta beleive this. Oh, phew! ME so Excitipated !!!!!
Let ME see - Haven't I told You yet ???
WELL ! ME FOUND ME GRAND-DAM !!
Yes!!!!!!!
A real, live, beautiful, black, happy, Grand-Dam!
And she is on the internet (bit GordonHelp here!)
Now let ME get this Right . [Lick left forepaw]
Her name is Bella,
Oh WOW - what a beautiful name for a Grand- Dam!
Her 'Sunday Name' is
Wizardwood RUSHING WATER at Tanglebriar
and . . . and . . and . . .

Today (Isn't it Always)

Steady on FollyThing!
Most of us had Grand-Dams at one time or another,
Nothing to it really . . .
You just look them up and there they are,
They tend to come in pairs.
Now boasting about your breeding
Is NOT the Done Thing
SOME of us have Breeding and others, do not
So we just do not mention it (we just KNOW!)
Now let me mention a much more important matter
All Dog People in the U.K. very upset Time Ago as
Government-Yucky-Thing ban selling 'Meat on Bone'
This mean no Marrow Bones - BUT
Government-Not-Quite-So-Yucky-Thing capitulates
Me had first Marrow Bone for TWO years
Me LAIR bone on Lawn - Crunch - Oooooooh!

TodayNow

GordonMate give ME FunnyThing
All Bloody-Sniff. Humph
Me has food COOKED, not uncooked!
Saga go all LAIR with her FunnyThing in Mouth
Me delicately take FunnyThing to LawnCorner
Keep eyeing Saga to see what SagaDo
Saga goes CrunchGrind on FunnyThing - Me try
Me Like It !! SagaSez called Marrow-Bone
Yipeeeee! me crunch first Marrow-Bone in life
SagSez me should sue Government-Yuck for compensation

But ME not know who Sue is . . .
Gordon gives me old mooring warp Today Ago Ago
Me use as new plaything
Mooring Warp about 30ft long
Me can drag it round house . . .
And out into garden . . .
And back into house
EVER SO FAST
GordonMate keep uprighting felled coffee tables
And rooting unrooted plants
GordonMate Yell at ME - but also fall about laughing
Gordon.laughing an yelling same time
Me chewing old warp like Marrow Bone - it shreds
MORE Yells!

Saga and Folly

21

LOG FOURTEEN

In which Saga appears to be going bonkers,
but comes into her own at a Flatcoat Fun Day,
whilst Folly performs an Heroic Rescue on
Coniston Water but worries about Growing Up!

Today (Isn't it Always)
ME in Big Trouble
GordonMate talking of ME need Pshycho-thingamy!
ME think Psycho-thingamy not for eating
Maybe but for BrainMessing
Gordon say ME not have enough brain-cells
For Psycho- thingamy, he say if he paid ME for
Psycho-thingamying by the number of my brain cells
Then he have to pay very few pennies
ME thinks this possibly an insult
But might be a Good Thing.

Anyhow-ways GordonMate think ME barmy
ME now Mature, Sensible Flatcoat Citizen so . .
why ME at NightSnoozeTime churn up Lino
I make it into tiny bits with ClawScrape.
Also ME go Pant/Shiver/Bolt at Medicine-Man-Vet?
Vet says "bring that Flatcoat in any time
We can give her a titbit so she gets to like us
ME NOT FOOL. If Vet-Man give ME titbit
 He also give ClawAmputate or StickInNeedle.
GordonMate say " he is a kind man"
She economical with truth!
ME cogitate at NightSnoozeTime
ME decide to ClawUp lino
 Just in case Medicine-Man-Vet come as Boogie!
Scrabble-Scrape-Pant-Slobber-Claw Ooooooh!

TodayNow

Me did a Very Good Thing TodayAgo!
Yes, Me!
A Good Thing!!!
Very Very windy day on Coniston Water
Much better day for Long Walk
Than for messing about in Gordon Boats
Gordon has GordonMate crewing for him on boat 'Ruskin'
Me and Saga do goooey-eye thing for Yankee-Doodles
All slobbery about us cos their dogs in Yankee-Doodle land
Well we get to Brantwood jetty
GordonMate jumps off boat and does warp-ey thing
BUT wind goes Wheeee-Bluster

GordonMate's smart Coniston launch hat goes Whoosh . .
Ends up in water longways from jetty
GordonMate distressed and cannot reach with boathook
Me jumps up and down
"Let me, Let me, LET ME"
Gordon very dopey (see bit about Brain Cells above)
At last he realises he has two RETRIEVERS to hand
Gordon takes me and SagaFriend and does 'Hi-Lost' thing
Water very rough so cannot see 'Hi-Lost'
Gordon makes SagaSit, he throws stone and says
"Folly, Hi-Lost me LEAP IN and SWIM STRONGLY
I FIND GordonMate Hat and Retrieve hat to stoney-shore
I have 'All-Over-GordonMate-S hake'
GordonMate pleased with me
She not say usual " Push-Off-You- Brat"

Today (Isn't it Always)

Gordon take ME and FollyThing to Flatcoat Fun Day
Gordon never been to before so he very uncertain
ME not sure he can do all ME want him to do
ME take him to Retrieve-The-Dummy competition
make sure he really understands what he has to do
Gordon think he is showing ME - Pwoooof!
ME make him stand still and give the 'Hi-Lost'
ME race over straw bales, sniff/grab dummy,
BUT Gordon moves so spoils ME retrieve.
ME does perfect jump-into-pen retrieve
Gordon say me had no training
So how can I do all these things?

Pshaw ! ME a Flatcoated Retriever!
ME take Gordon to Flyball training
Gordon has to run over jumps with tennis ball
 VERY FUNNY SIGHT!
ME do well with retrieving tennis balls BUT
Gordon gets all Uppity-Tetchy about ME
Because ME is expected to paw for ball
ME had whole thing sussed anyways
ME go round back and face-lick BallTenderMan
He upset, say I need more training
Gordon and GordonWasPup called Greg
take ME to Obedience Ring with FollyThing
ME Very Good Sit/Stay/Heel
Nice Man has chewy-bits - very yummy - Ooooooh!

TodayNow

Me very muchly miffed at Fun Day
GordonWasPup's Girlfriend take me to Rather Old Man
Rather Old Man has big slideystickthing
Puts slideystickthing over me shoulder
Me has little wriggle just to show who is Boss
Rather Old Man hasslideystickthing and is Very Serious
hH talk to Gordon
He say "Folly is outside the Breed Standard, she is too tall"
Me upset
Not me fault me too tall
Me do my best
Everwhichperson in me wholelife saying "Grow Up, Folly"
Well me tried everso hard to Grow Up

Now look what's happened - me Overgrown Up!
Me over twenty four inches at shoulder
SagaFriend just twenty two and three quarters
Rather Old Man say "Saga perfect for bitch"
Me think life Very Unfair
Me think going to Flatcoat FunDay is GordonRuse
Me think Gordon just want to drive new Alfa-car
Me go and dream-retrieve a few more hats to feel better

Saga and Folly

ABOUT THE AUTHOR

Dogs have been my companions since my earliest days. My first memories are of a huge (relative to a very small me!) Labrador called Peter Boy. My father had a 'thing' about Labradors, hence a procession of Tulip, Merry, Gay, Gambol and Ace. My mother at one stage struck out independently with a Pointer called Heather. My parents also owned a pack of hunting Beagles (The Wimbish).

When I settled down and married we also started down the Labrador route, with Whimsey, then to a Golden retriever, Fable, before finding Flatcoats were the 'Very Best' of breeds with Saga, Folly and Epic.

Whilst all this important dog-stuff was happening I qualified as a Land Agent and worked in Norfolk and Northumberland before joining the National Trust and working as their regional Agent in North Wales and the Lake District. It all became (probably rightly) a bit too corporate for me and I left and established a passenger boat business on Coniston Water, which I sold just before the recession.

I now live in northern Greece where I find the climate rather less friendly than England, but the people somewhat more so.